DARLINGTON'S MARGARET

by Dorothy Hodgkins

Dorothy Hodgkins ☺

Trafford
PUBLISHING®

Order this book online at www.trafford.com/08-1168
or email orders@trafford.com

Most Trafford titles are also available at major online book retailers.

Note for Librarians: A cataloguing record for this book is available from Library
and Archives Canada at www.collectionscanada.ca/amicus/index-e.html

Printed in Victoria, BC, Canada.

ISBN: 978-1-4251-8668-5

*We at Trafford believe that it is the responsibility of us all, as both individuals and corporations,
to make choices that are environmentally and socially sound. You, in turn, are supporting this
responsible conduct each time you purchase a Trafford book, or make use of our publishing services.
To find out how you are helping, please visit www.trafford.com/responsiblepublishing.html*

*Our mission is to efficiently provide the world's finest, most comprehensive book publishing
service, enabling every author to experience success. To find out how to publish your book, your
way, and have it available worldwide, visit us online at www.trafford.com/10510*

 www.trafford.com

North America & international
toll-free: 1 888 232 4444 (USA & Canada)
phone: 250 383 6864 • fax: 250 383 6804 • email: info@trafford.com

The United Kingdom & Europe
phone: +44 (0)1865 487 395 • local rate: 0845 230 9601
facsimile: +44 (0)1865 481 507 • email: info.uk@trafford.com

10 9 8 7 6 5 4 3

Dedication

This book is written to celebrate my mother, who would tell me stories of her childhood at bedtime and sing me to sleep at night.

Out on the ocean
carved on a rock
are three little words
forget-me-not

Anonymous

Illustrations

Contents

Old Homestead, Darlington, England

CHAPTER 1

On the Ocean

TWELVE-YEAR-OLD MARGARET COOK leaned against the cold steel railing of the ship, watching the British coastline fade away in the distance. The sky and sea blurred together like a gray wool blanket had been tossed over everything. Margaret felt suffocated. An ocean wave splashed against the hull, sending salt water straight up in the air. Margaret felt the spray rain down on her cheeks and mix with her tears. Tipped off balance by a sudden movement of the ship, she slipped and banged her arm. "Ow," she said, rubbing it and trying to steady herself.

The Captain approached Margaret and placed a protective hand on her shoulder. "These rough seas could wash you overboard, Margaret. Go change into dry clothes. I don't want you to become ill."

Margaret nodded her head and walked unsteadily to her cabin. Her sister, nine-year-old Beth lay moaning on one of the bunks. She was seasick and Margaret thought homesick as well.

"Can I get you anything, Beth?"

"No, thank you. I just need to lay here for a while. What happened to your arm?"

"It's a bit sore. I banged it on the railing."

Margaret opened her trunk and pulled out her favorite sweater. The smell of home still lingered with the smell of soap and she took a deep breath. While she changed into dry clothes, she noticed EVERY GIRL'S ANNUAL peeking at her from the bottom of the trunk. She reached down to pick it up. A figure skater graced the outside cover of the book and on the inside, her mother had written, "Christmas 1946. To my darling Margaret with love from Mam."

Margaret repeated the words in her mind and closed her eyes.

The events leading up to this moment had been unexpected and confusing. Father had drowned while on a fishing trip at the age of 34. His death left their invalid mother with four children and no income. Mam sold the house and made arrangements to send her three oldest children to Canada, thinking the children would be better off living with their elderly great aunt. Canada seemed like the Promised Land after the Second World War, a place with advantages not available in England.

On January 12, 1948, Margaret, Beth and her brother Tom had stood beside their mother's bed for the last time while Mam prayed for them and held each one tightly, kissing them and telling them she loved them.

It was Aunt Freda who accompanied them to Liverpool to board the freight ship named the Cairnavon and had stood at the dock waving until their ship was out of sight.

A knock on the cabin door interrupted Margaret's thoughts. She put her book back in the trunk and closed the lid.

"Hello?" she said, opening the door.

"My name's Curley. I'm here to escort you to dinner with the Captain." His green eyes sparkled and his bright red hair was wind blown. He was six feet tall, tanned and muscular.

Margaret realized she was staring and felt foolish. "I don't think we'll be able to come. Beth's not feeling well and I should stay with her."

Beth scrambled from her bed and hurried to the door. "I'm feeling better now."

"Are you sure?" Margaret asked, looking at Beth's pale face.

"Yes," she said.

"I'll wait for you out here," Curley said.

Margaret nodded, "We won't be long."

Margaret glanced in the mirror, made her best smile and tried to hold it in place while Beth brushed her own hair furiously trying to fluff up what had been flattened in bed and tangled by the wind.

"Come on," Margaret encouraged. "We don't want to keep him waiting."

The girls walked shyly beside Curley as he chatted with them along the way.

The Captain's dining room was spotlessly clean. All the chrome was shining and the red mahogany table in the center of the room was highly polished. Margaret chose a chair to the left of her brother Tom and Beth sat to his right. Margaret wanted to move her chair forward a bit but it was bolted to the floor. The three children sat on the edge of their seats waiting expectantly for something to happen.

Margaret was proud to see Tom looking his best in slicked back black hair and clean, wrinkle free clothes.

"Welcome, children. We seldom have passengers and Curley needs a break from the routine. I've assigned him to look after your needs during your two week stay."

Tom spoke up quickly, "Thank you, Captain."

The Captain introduced them to other passengers who were traveling with them.

Jenny was a young actress moving to New York City. "Come visit me in my cabin if you want," she said smiling. "I have a younger sister about your age. It will keep me from being lonely."

Margaret and Beth promised to visit her.

Sam the cook pushed a cart into the room and served dinner to everyone at once. Margaret was starting to feel hungry. She touched the warm plate in front of her and lifted the stainless steel cover. Steam rushed out and a delicious aroma escaped. She stared at a thick slice of roast beef, bright orange buttered carrots and mashed potatoes with dark brown gravy and her mouth watered. "Yum!" she said.

"Hold onto your dishes while you eat, children," Sam warned. "If the waves are choppy, the ship will move and your food will slide into your laps."

"Is that why the table and chairs are bolted to the floor?" Beth asked.

"Yes," the cook replied. "The cupboards are locked for the same reason."

After dinner, the children helped clear the table. Sam was impressed with their behavior. "I could use some help in the galley."

"I want to help," Beth offered eagerly.

"Me, too." Margaret agreed.

The cook started gathering up the dishes and the girls began to help him when the Captain interrupted them.

"I'd like to give the children a tour of the ship, Sam. I'll send them back to you when we're finished."

Sam nodded, "Thanks for your help, children. I'll prepare a snack for you when you return."

The Captain walked with them to the control room. "Stand over here and I'll explain how everything works." He showed them dials, handles and machinery, telling each function and finishing his tour by explaining the steering mechanism. "When this brass knob is not held in the correct position, the wind and waves push us off course. A few degrees to the left or right can mean hundreds of miles in the wrong direction."

Margaret stared out the window, imagining them sailing to some exotic deserted island, but then her Great Aunt would be worried about them. This ended the fantasy and she watched as the Captain let Tom take the helm. After this, Margaret and Beth each took a turn steering the ship.

"Curley will guide you on a tour of the rest of the ship as I have other duties to perform. No area is off limits as long as you follow safety guidelines."

The children thanked the Captain and followed Curley up a steel staircase to the radio room where an operator was clicking messages in Morse code to passing ships. They climbed down into the hold, walked along a catwalk and stopped to watch an engineer shovel coal into a big furnace.

Curley walked with them back to the galley, "The cook will get you a snack now. I have to write a report for the Captain. As soon as I've finished, I'll return and take you to see the games room."

"Bye for now," Margaret said. "We'll see you later."

"Curley's cute," Beth whispered to Margaret.

"I wonder how old he is," Margaret answered.

"Tom. Do you know how old Curley is?" Beth asked.

"He's two years older than me. Sixteen. Why? Are you in love with him?" he teased.

Beth blushed, "What if I am? It's no concern of yours!"

Tom admired the brass gong hanging on the wall by the door and when the cook entered the room, he asked about it.

"Do you use this gong or is it just a decoration?"

The cook picked up a small hammer and tapped it lightly. A loud clear note vibrated through the room.

"That's loud," Margaret shouted, covering her ears.

The cook quickly put his hand out to stop the noise.

"We use this gong to summon the crew or give specific orders. It's loud enough to be heard anywhere on the ship. Would you like to take turns hitting the gong at mealtime?"

"Can I be first?" Beth asked eagerly.

"Yes. Come back tomorrow at 11:00 to announce lunch."

Curley poked his head through the doorway, "Are you ready to go to the games room?"

"Sure," Tom answered.

"Beth and I want to visit Jenny," Margaret said apologizing. "We can see the games room another time."

"Come on, Tom," Curley said. "I think a game of darts is waiting for us."

After the boys left, Beth turned to Margaret. "Why don't you want to go with them?"

"I think Tom will enjoy his time with Curley more without us tagging along. Besides, I'd like to visit Jenny."

Beth walked with Margaret to Jenny's cabin. Margaret knocked and Jenny invited them in.

"Hi," Margaret said as she and Beth entered her cabin.

"Hello, girls," she answered. "I was hoping you'd come to visit me."

The girls talked with Jenny about clothes, acting and what it was like growing up during the war. "It must be pretty hard leaving your mother behind. I know what cheers me up," Jenny said. "Would you let me style your hair and would you like to try on some of my dresses?"

"That would be fun," Margaret answered eagerly. She noticed how pretty Jenny's brown hair was and wondered if her hair could be styled to look the same.

After Jenny experimented with their hair for a while, she chose clothes to suit each girl.

Margaret wore a green blouse and Beth admired her rust colored sweater in the mirror. "We look pretty good even if the clothes are a bit baggy," Margaret exclaimed. Her big brown eyes appeared larger with make-up and her rosy cheeks glowed with rouge. Her wavy hair was tied back with a ribbon and wispy curls framed her face.

Jenny had pinned Beth's hair in small curls around her head like Shirley Temple. "Let's show the boys," she said excitedly.

Emily Cook (Mam)

"You can keep the clothes for the evening and bring them back to me in the morning," Jenny said.

Margaret and Beth found the boys playing darts in the games room.

"How do we look?" Margaret asked.

Curley and Tom turned to look with half interest.

Beth shook her blond curls and stood with her hands on her hips waiting.

Curley cleared his throat several times. "You look nice," he said, "Both of you." Suddenly, his skin turned red from his neck to his ears.

Tom laughed, "Your hair looks nice but your clothes are funny. I think you look like clowns."

Margaret blushed and Beth pinched his arm.

"Stop. Stop," he laughed, "I like clowns."

Beth pinched him again before she stomped away with Margaret close behind.

Margaret pulled the ribbon out of her hair and ran her fingers through it.

"Brothers," Beth announced loudly. "You should have left your hair up. I'm going to leave mine the way it is until bedtime. I don't care what Tom says about it."

Margaret shrugged, "I feel embarrassed."

"You heard what Curley said, he said we look nice. What do brothers know?" Beth answered, grinning at Margaret.

Two weeks on board slipped by quickly. The crew felt like family and Margaret had become attached to them. The girls had spent many hours with Jenny and they had become good friends. Margaret knew it would be hard to say good-bye. "Will we be forever leaving those we love?" she thought. The last night on board she stood on deck staring at the millions of stars shining in the night sky and thinking perhaps her mother was looking at the same stars.

"Will I be happy in Canada? Will I ever return to England? How old will I be? What if I get married? Will Mam be alive to meet my husband? Will I ever see Mam or baby Gordon again?"

That night they sailed into the Bay of Fundy. A tugboat arrived to escort the Cairnavon through the shallow water to the docks in St. John, New Brunswick. The children stood on board looking with wonder at the lights of the city and lots and lots of snow. They were soon chilly and went to their cabins to pack.

The next morning was Beth's tenth birthday. The cook prepared a special breakfast followed by bowls of strawberries and hot chocolate fondue for dipping. Several of the crew approached the children during the morning to shake their hands. Margaret tried to be cheerful.

The Captain walked with the children onto the dock to wait for the two Red Cross officials who would accompany them to their great aunt's.

"I f-feel dizzy," Margaret said holding Beth's arm and shivering. "The ground is moving b-back and forth."

"You are 'land-sick'," the Captain observed. "You're used to the movement of the ship. It will take time for your body to adjust. How do you like the snow? It's always like this in the winter."

Margaret and Beth were standing close together. Tom had his shoulders hunched and his hands jammed into his pockets. "It's p-p-pretty but very c-c-cold," Margaret said as her teeth chattered.

"Your escorts are here," the Captain said, "Good-bye, children. I enjoyed having you aboard. I hope your stay in Canada will be a happy one."

He whispered something to the Red Cross officials and shook the children's hands. They waved to him as he walked back to the ship.

Margaret felt like she was being thrown from one situation into another without the chance to deal with either of them. Things were happening too fast.

"Hi, my name is Ken and this is Linda. We work for the Red Cross. Your Great Aunt Aileen has arranged for us to travel with you on the train to Welland, Ontario. Let's put your luggage in the trunk," he said, lifting one of their trunks and putting it in the "trunk". Margaret found his speech confusing.

Everyone got into the car. Margaret was horrified to see Ken driving on the wrong side of the road. At every turn, her stomach lurched. She expected to meet another car head-on. "I think I'm going to be sick," she announced.

"I'll pull over to the side of the road for a few minutes," Ken announced.

Linda looked with concern at Margaret. "Are you feeling better?"

"We drive on the opposite side of the street in England. I'm not feeling any better," she answered, "but keep driving. The sooner we're out of the car the better."

Ken and Linda parked in front of a store. "We have time to shop before the train arrives," Ken said to Linda.

"We don't have any spending money," Tom said frowning.

"You won't need any," Linda explained. "Ken and I are going to buy you warm coats and snow pants."

Margaret was surprised. "You don't have to do that. We can get sweaters out of our trunks."

"We want to do it," Linda said.

After Margaret changed into her new winter clothes, she felt toasty warm. "I wonder if all Canadians will be as generous as the Red Cross has been," she said to Beth.

They stopped at a restaurant and ordered hot soup and biscuits. By the end of the meal, all three children felt warm but tired. Tom's face was white, Beth looked wilted and Margaret was having a hard time staying awake. Margaret wished they didn't have a long train trip ahead of them.

Linda handed a parcel wrapped in pretty paper to Beth, "This is for your birthday."

"How did you know?" she asked. Beth unwrapped the parcel to find a shiny black purse. "I think its leather. Look at all the compartments. Thank you so much!" she said happily.

After lunch, they drove to the Canadian National Railway station.

Ken and Linda located the sleeping car and the berths they would use overnight. Margaret was glad they had the car to themselves.

Margaret was too nervous to sleep soundly. Besides, she heard many creaks and rattles and groans as the train sped down the track. Her mind raced with thoughts about her mother and fear about what would happen when they arrived at their destination.

She missed the crew of the Cairnavon. "I hope we meet them again," she thought.

When the train arrived in Toronto, they switched to the THB Railway (Toronto, Hamilton and Buffalo), to ride in a passenger car the rest of the way to Welland, Ontario.

Ken and Linda bought strawberry ice cream and Margaret wondered how she could enjoy eating something cold when it was so cold outside, but it was warm in the train and it helped her feel better. Tom didn't eat any of the ice cream because he was feeling sick.

Margaret looked through the window and counted telephone poles until they stopped briefly in Hamilton. Before they reached the city limits, the train whistle sounded.

"We're almost there," Linda informed them. Margaret's stomach felt full of butterflies as they pulled into the Welland Train Station on King Street.

She searched for a familiar face among the crowd and found one. Without having met her great aunt before or seeing a recent photograph of her, Margaret recognized her immediately. A feeling of dread came over her. Aunt Aileen was old and cross looking. She was not smiling and resembled her short-tempered sister, Great Aunt Brenda in England. Margaret looked at Beth and saw her mouth open.

Beth turned to look at Margaret. "Oh, no!" she said.

Great Aunt Aileen

CHAPTER 2

A Cold Welcome

AILEEN DAVIS ELBOWED her way through a gathering crowd of people to reach the children. A man with a camera took a picture of them together while a reporter from the Evening Tribune briefly interviewed them.

Margaret felt bewildered. She closed her eyes and rubbed her forehead.

Ken spoke loudly to the crowd, "Can't you see how tired they are? Let's find a place for them to sit down."

The reporter directed most of his questions to Tom.

"How did you like the ocean trip?"

"Okay," said Tom, "I wouldn't mind another one."

"Do you find Canada cold?"

"It's not too bad but back in England, the grass is green and daffodils and other spring flowers are coming out."

"How did you enjoy the train trip?"

"I thought we'd never get here. I was sick on the train. The girls were all right. They got to eat ice-cream."

"What's the first thing you'd like to do, now you are in Canada?"

"I hope I have the chance to go skating," Tom replied.

Margaret and Beth nodded their heads in agreement.

"Miss Davis, do you have anything to add?"

Aunt Aileen replied, "I wish I could have met them at the boat in New Brunswick."

Aunt Aileen hailed a taxi and climbed in the front seat while motioning for the children to get into the back. Her house was only a few blocks from the train station and they arrived in a short time.

At first glance, the boarding house on Hellems Avenue looked inviting and impressive. It was three stories high, an ancient structure in good repair with many tall windows and an elaborately carved wooden railing that circled a front veranda.

Snow-covered box hedges outlined the property and elm trees lined both sides of the sidewalk leading to the front step. Old rose vines grew tangled around trellises on both sides of the veranda.

"I can't wait to see your garden in the spring, Auntie," Margaret said.

Aunt Aileen ignored Margaret. She reached into her purse, counted out 30 cents and paid the driver. The children climbed out of the taxi and waited while he unloaded the trunks beside the curb.

Aunt Aileen did not attempt to help the children carry their possessions to the house. The children struggled into the front hall and set them down. The smell of furniture polish and floor cleaner met them at the entrance to the dining room.

"Tom, your bedroom is in the basement down those stairs. Margaret and Beth, follow me up to the second floor."

Tom helped the girls by lifting one of the trunks up the stairs. Margaret and Beth each took an end of the other one and carried it together. Because it was heavy, they had to set it down several times.

Aunt Aileen tapped her foot impatiently and examined the hardwood floor for scratches every time they did this.

Margaret looked gratefully at Tom, "Thank you."

"You're welcome."

Aunt Aileen cleared her throat for attention. "The five bedrooms are occupied by boarders. You must enter the rooms once a day to dust the furniture and change the linens. Only do this when the boarders are absent. All other times, the rooms are off limits.

"You may store your empty trunks in one of the two large attic bedrooms until required by guests. This door stays locked at all times. Behind it is a stairway leading to my bedroom. You are not allowed to use these stairs even if you find the door unlocked.

"You will share this washroom with your mother's sister Rose as well as myself. Rose is away visiting friends and will return Monday night."

At the end of the hall was an enclosed porch. Windows filled one wall from floor to ceiling. The room was not heated.

"This is your bedroom. Prepare for bed. I'll call on you every morning at 6:00 a.m." Aunt Aileen left the girls and motioned for Tom to accompany her downstairs.

Margaret watched Aunt Aileen walk down the hall, "Whatever happened to the simple courtesy of 'Hello' or 'How do you do?'" Beth nodded her head in agreement.

Margaret shrugged. "Let's see what kind of view there is." She pulled aside the curtains to look out. Frost formed interesting designs on the inside of the window. A patch of mould grew on the ledge where some moisture had seeped in.

"We'd better tell Auntie about the mould," she said.

"Children are to be seen and not heard," Beth countered. "You know the old saying, I doubt if she'll listen to anything we say."

Margaret nodded and began to unpack. Margaret shivered as she picked out what she would wear in the morning. She folded her clothes neatly and put them under the blankets at the foot of her bed. "I want them to be warm when I put them on in the morning."

She picked up her nightgown, "I'm going to change under the covers."

"That's a good idea," Beth agreed.

Margaret climbed under the covers and struggled into her nightgown, "It's harder than I thought," she said. "But at least I'm getting warm with the effort," she mumbled.

The low light in the hall crept into their bedroom and Margaret could see her breath. The room smelled musty from disuse. Margaret lay for a while trying not to breathe in the odor. It was soon replaced by the smell of mothballs as she pulled the covers tight over her head. She blew into her pillow, making a warm spot to rest her cheek on, and fell asleep.

A few hours later, Beth whispered to Margaret, "I'm freezing. Can I climb in bed with you?"

Margaret stirred slightly, "Yes. If you want to."

Beth climbed down from the top bunk in less than a second.

She pulled the covers back and a rush of cold air hit Margaret.

"Hurry. I'm getting cold."

Beth put her cold feet on Margaret's leg and Margaret screamed. Margaret instantly covered her mouth.

"SHH! Auntie will hear you," Beth whispered.

"I couldn't help it," whispered Margaret. She listened for footsteps outside the door. After several minutes she sighed with relief.

Beth soon fell asleep. Margaret thought about the reason she had come to Canada. Her mother wished for Margaret to remain in England to help with baby Gordon but Margaret couldn't bear to be parted from Beth. She could imagine how hard it would have been for Beth to sleep here alone and was glad she had come. She hoped Tom didn't mind sleeping in the basement. That first night, Margaret and Beth held hands while they slept.

It seemed to Margaret as if she had just fallen asleep when she heard a tapping sound on the door. Opening it a crack, she was startled by the unfamiliar face of Aunt Aileen peering at her.

The sour expression made Auntie look menacing and she pointed a crooked finger at Margaret that frightened her.

"You're late, it's 6:10 in the morning and Mr. Booth has to leave by 6:30."

There was no time to wash. They dressed quickly and thumped

down the stairs, wiping the sleep from their eyes.

Auntie grabbed Margaret's arm. "Do not run in my house," she said angrily. "I hope you know how to cook."

Margaret felt disappointed. She had hoped Auntie's grumpy attitude was because she wasn't feeling well but it appeared to be her normal behavior. She walked quickly to the kitchen and searched for a pot to boil water.

"That's the wrong pan. Use this pan for oatmeal and don't forget. I don't tolerate mistakes."

When Auntie left the kitchen, Margaret looked at Beth and rolled her eyes. Beth looked back with a sorry expression as she prepared the tea.

Margaret carried the prepared oatmeal to the table and Beth carried the tea. Mr. Booth looked sternly at the children and at his watch, showing his disapproval of them.

It seemed to Margaret, however, the other boarders noticed their discomfort and were trying to make up for it.

One man commented, "Thank you for this fine breakfast."

Another said, "You did an excellent job."

One young woman said, "This is the best oatmeal I've ever tasted."

Margaret felt like laughing at this because, after all, oatmeal is oatmeal.

Margaret and Beth handed out packed lunches to various boarders before clearing the table and washing the dishes.

Tom carried armfuls of chopped wood to the basement and they heard him thump down the stairs. A short while later, he returned with a sack of potatoes. He opened one end and began to peel them.

Beth reset the table for dinner and helped Margaret dry and put away breakfast dishes.

Only after these chores were finished were they allowed to eat their own breakfast and Aunt Aileen told them what they could eat and what they could not eat.

"The butter is for the boarders," Auntie said. "The fresh bread is for the boarders. They pay good money for that food and you are not to eat it. You can have the other bread."

The "other bread" was slightly stale and Margaret wondered if it would always be this way. Aunt Aileen seemed wealthy enough to feed them properly if she wanted to.

Margaret made up her mind to enjoy her meals and wear a cheerful smile. "Auntie isn't going to make me miserable if I can help it," she said to herself.

"How did you sleep last night, Tom?" Margaret asked. "We were cold."

"I have it better than you can imagine. My bed is warm next to the furnace. In the fruit cellar, I discovered where she keeps her canning."

He showed them an empty can of peaches.

Margaret grabbed it and stuffed it in the bottom of the garbage bin, underneath some old papers. "Be careful," She said looking worried.

"Aunt Aileen can't be everywhere at once," Tom said. "We can help each other in many ways without her knowing about it."

Several days passed, and one morning, after the beds were stripped, the girls carried the dirty laundry down to the basement and saw Tom stacking wood.

"I hope she enrolls us in school soon," Tom commented to Margaret. "I have no privacy down here after 6:00 in the morning and since we're not allowed in the dining area or the living room, there's no place for me to go. I'm getting bored."

Aunt Aileen came to check on the girls' progress and prodded them to work faster.

After the laundry, the girls went back upstairs. Margaret was talking to herself while changing the sheets on one of the beds when Aunt Aileen appeared out of nowhere and grabbed Margaret's sleeve.

"You ungrateful child! Go to your room and stay there."

Beth checked on Margaret after Auntie went down to the kitchen.

"I saw Auntie sneak up the back stairs to spy on you. She was wearing soft-soled shoes and walking very slowly."

"She must have heard me complaining."

Beth looked surprised. "You never complain about anything."

"Well, I didn't mean for anyone to hear me. I was just saying whatever came to mind."

After that, Margaret discovered she had to be careful what she said even if her Aunt was away shopping. Aunt Aileen confronted Margaret about something she and Beth had been discussing outside Mr. Booth's bedroom. Mr. Booth told Auntie everything they said.

"You never know who's listening," she said to Beth. "Auntie makes me feel like a criminal."

Margaret had started out with the intention of treating Aunt Aileen as she would her own mother. She would say "Good-night" and approach her for a hug, but her Aunt either pushed her away or stood stiff and unyielding with her face turned away.

Margaret felt sorry for Aunt Aileen and wondered how she could have any friends, but when her Aunt made unkind remarks about Margaret's mother with guests present, and even with Margaret standing in the same room, she felt very angry.

"How dare she say such things about Mam. She only wants us here to do her work for her," Margaret thought angrily.

After the children were familiar with the daily routine, Aunt Aileen enrolled them at Central School on Division Street, around the corner from their house. Margaret sighed with relief.

Margaret, Tom and Beth at Niagara Falls

CHAPTER 3

Fresh Breezes Blowing

$\mathcal{M}$ ISS WEBB STOOD at the front of the class. "Please stand for our national anthem, "God Save the Queen."

It was Monday morning. Margaret pushed her chair back and stood proudly. This was her national anthem too.

A carelessly placed book slid off the edge of a desk and fell with a bang to the floor. She watched a girl bend down to pick it up while the boy next to her kicked it away. The girl frowned and stood up again.

"Today we welcome two new students from Darlington, England. Please make them feel at home," the teacher began. "Beginning on my left, each of you tell Margaret and Tom Cook your name and something interesting about yourselves."

"Hi, my name is Lydia and I like horseback riding."

By the time all the students were finished introducing themselves, Math class was half over. Miss Webb used the remainder of her time to review lessons she had taught from the start of the year. She handed out assignments and took Margaret and Tom aside to teach them the Canadian money.

In History class, Margaret didn't understand what Miss Webb was talking about. Her choice of words, their meanings and pronunciation were unfamiliar to Margaret. When Miss Webb wrote information on the blackboard, Margaret had to squint to see it. She became bored and imagined herself back in England. Her ears picked up the teacher's voice as a buzzing sound in the background and the tapping of chalk at irregular intervals almost put her to sleep. She began to hum.

Margaret heard her name spoken quietly as if from a great distance away, "Margaret, Margaret!" She looked up to see Miss Webb standing over her. "Margaret!"

Margaret was embarrassed, "Yes, Miss Webb."

"Please stop humming."

Miss Webb was impressed with the style of writing Margaret had learned in Britain and asked her to write her name on the blackboard.

"Students. This is quality penmanship. I expect the same from each of you."

At the end of the day, Margaret found herself surrounded by a friendly group of girls.

"Hi, I'm Jessica Miller. We're going skating on the weekend and you can come with us if you want. I'll come by and pick you up at 3:00 on Saturday afternoon," Jessica volunteered.

"My Aunt won't allow me to have friends over to the house and I'm not sure my chores will be done by then."

"I'll stop by anyway, just in case."

"Thanks, Jessica."

Margaret and Tom walked together to the other end of the school building, looking for Beth.

"I hope Beth isn't lonely," Margaret said.

"Don't worry," Tom said pointing.

A large group of children surrounded Beth. They were gesturing and laughing. When she started to walk toward Margaret and Tom, some followed her, patting her back and chatting excitedly.

Margaret was glad to see Beth accepted by the other students her age. She had worried about her all morning.

A cold wet snowball hit her in the neck and water trickled down her shirt. She looked up to see a dozen or more snowballs of various sizes sailing in her direction. She quickly scooped up snow and flung it at the nearest attacker. Tom and several boys joined in the fight and for twenty minutes, snow flew everywhere. Finally, the group broke up and the children walked home.

That evening, after they had gone to bed, Margaret heard a sound in her room. Startled, she sat up suddenly to see what appeared to be her mother's face bending over her. "Mam?!"

"No, Margaret. I'm your Aunt Rose. But you can just call me Rose. I'll see you in the morning." She kissed Margaret on the cheek and bent over Beth to do the same. The sweet smell of lilacs swept through the room and followed her out the door. Margaret lay awake for a long time with tears streaming down her cheeks, feeling both sad and excited.

Margaret liked Rose immediately. She had the same manners as Mam, only mixed with a bit of mischief. When Aunt Aileen treated Margaret or Beth unfairly; Rose did something nice for them to make up for it. She brought them candy when Aunt Aileen was out shopping and helped them do their chores. She always left the last thing on the list for the children to do so Aunt Aileen would find them working when she returned.

On Thursday, Aunt Aileen made soup. She forgot to soak the beans overnight and didn't see the dead bugs floating in it.

"Aunt Aileen, I know you have to go out tonight. Why don't you get ready? I'll prepare tea and help the children clear the table," Rose offered.

"Thank you, Rose. That will save me some time."

As soon as Auntie left the room, Rose whispered to Margaret, "Don't eat the soup. Carry it to the back door."

Rose took the beans and dumped them on the compost heap. She quickly made the children some cheese sandwiches. They were still eating when Auntie returned to the kitchen.

Aunt Aileen looked suspiciously at the children, "What's going on here?"

"They're still hungry and I made them a snack," Rose answered quickly.

Rose carried tea into the living room for Aunt Aileen and Margaret watched Aunt Aileen sit down to drink it.

Margaret finished clearing the table and turned to Tom, "That was a close call."

"Well, if she saw your cheeks," commented Tom, "she's sure to know something is up. You're as red as a beet."

Saturday morning Margaret woke before the alarm. The sun was beating through the curtains heating up the room and birds were chirping loudly in the trees outside the window.

Margaret got up and looked out the window. Some of the snow had melted. "I wonder if the ice will still be thick enough for skating," she thought.

Margaret yawned. "Beth, are you awake?"

"I am now."

"Sorry."

"I was awake before. I'm just kidding. What do you want?"

"Do you remember the night we met Rose?"

Beth nodded her head. "Doesn't she remind you of Mam?"

"I know. When I thought it was Mam leaning over me, I almost choked," Margaret replied.

"She looks so young, but she's over thirty. Remember what Mam says, how a smile makes you look younger," Beth remarked.

"Aunt Rose will always seem young because she is always smiling," Margaret concluded.

When Margaret finished breakfast, Auntie gave her a long list of cleaning duties. "I doubt I can finish this before Jessica arrives," she complained to herself. "There's no chance of my going skating now."

Bending over a bucket of hot soapy water, she moved a scrub brush lightly across the hardwood floor. The scent of pine was overpowering. The doorbell rang and she opened the door. A man came in and hung his hat on a peg.

"Hello, I'm Jack Patterson," he said winking at Margaret. He walked straight toward Auntie's favorite chair and sat in it.

Shortly after this, Margaret heard a loud scratchy voice and a big woman came barging in, banging the door behind her. "Hello, Aileen," she announced loudly. "Put on the tea." She frowned at Margaret and walked right across the wet floor.

Margaret saw Auntie's face appear from the kitchen doorway, turning several shades of red, "Hello, Edie, Jack. Have a seat. I'll be in shortly."

"We thought we might take the children out for the day but I see they haven't finished their chores yet. We'll take them out next weekend," Edie announced. "How does a trip to Niagara Falls sound, eh?" she glanced in Margaret's general direction.

Margaret watched in amazement as Aunt Aileen rushed to the kitchen to prepare the tea.

Margaret went over the footprints again with a wet rag and began polishing the woodwork. After a short break for a sandwich, she started dusting. She was halfway through her chores when the doorbell rang. Aunt Aileen got up to answer it herself.

"Hello. Can Margaret come skating?"

Aunt Aileen looked past Jessica and frowned at Ted and Steve, the two boys waiting at the curb. "I don't think..."

Edie Patterson interrupted, "I don't think Margaret should have to do any more work for today. Go get your skates, Margaret. You need fresh air and exercise."

Margaret stood still with her mouth hanging open. Her cleaning rag slipped from her grasp and she looked back and forth between Edie Patterson and Aunt Aileen.

"Don't stand there looking stupid, Margaret," Aunt Aileen said sharply, "Put away the cleaning things and get moving!"

Margaret flashed a quick smile at Mrs. Patterson and hurried to put away the cleaning supplies before her Aunt could change her mind. She dressed in warm clothes and Rose handed her a couple sandwiches. She was almost out the door when she heard Aunt Aileen call out, "Be back by 6:00."

A large patch of ice on the Welland Canal had been shoveled off and twenty or more kids were skating around. The ice was smooth and Margaret felt nervous climbing down the bank. One of the boys named Ted took her hand and helped her down onto the ice. Jessica and her boyfriend climbed down and the two skated off. A gust of wind almost knocked Margaret over when she stepped onto the ice surface. Ted held her hand and they let the wind blow them across the ice to the opposite bank. Jessica and Steve soon joined them and the four children skated back toward the center where a human chain was formed to play crack the whip.

"There's Betty," commented Jessica. "She'll be the next Barbara Ann Scott!"

"Show us some of your figure skating moves," Jessica shouted.

Betty performed figure eights and twirled around. She started to show off a bit and talked some girls into attempting a stunt with her. Each girl placed their hands on the waist of the girl ahead of her and together they started to skate down the ice. "Everyone lift their right leg at the count of three."

"I don't think that's a good idea," Margaret whispered.

"Let's see what happens," Jessica answered.

As soon as the girls' legs went up, they fell like dominoes.

Fortunately, no one was hurt. A roar of laughter went up from a group of kids playing hockey and several boys came running to see if they needed help.

"Are you O.K. Betty?" one of them asked as he extended his hand to help her.

"I will be now. Thank you for helping me up," she answered.

Margaret and Jessica stayed for several hours. After pausing for a sandwich break, they decided it was time to go home. They found a bench and unlaced their skates. Ted and Steve decided to stay and play hockey. They waved goodbye and went to join the game.

"I'm getting cold. Would you like to stop at my house on the way home for a cup of hot chocolate?" Jessica asked.

"I'd love to," Margaret answered. "Thanks for being so friendly to me."

"I enjoy your company."

They arrived at Jessica's house and Mrs. Miller took their coats and hats. "Have a seat in the living room."

Jessica brought in cups of hot chocolate with marshmallows floating in them. Margaret took a sip and creamy bubbles stuck to her upper lip. She licked it off and smiled. "Yum."

"Hey, I think Mrs. Patterson has your Aunt Aileen wrapped around her little finger," Jessica said.

"You think she will do anything Edie says? It seems that way to me too. If it wasn't for Edie, I'd still be scrubbing floors or carrying out the garbage or finishing some other chores on my list. I expect I'll still have to do them when I get home."

Sure enough, as soon as she opened the door, Aunt Aileen confronted her.

"Here's the lazy girl. I've made a new list of chores for you to do." She handed Margaret a list twice as long as before.

Margaret shrugged. "I wonder what she means by that," she thought. "I go out of my way trying to please her."

"I hope she doesn't expect me to do everything tonight," Margaret told Rose. "Some of these jobs are repeats." She pointed at 'scrub and polish the floor'.

Aunt Rose looked at the list, "Help prepare dinner and ignore everything else, but if she tells you to do something Margaret, do it."

Beth and Margaret in front of home in Welland

Sunday morning Margaret dressed for church. Aunt Aileen was a member of Holy Trinity Church and it was within walking distance. Margaret recognized some of her friends from school. They invited her to become part of the youth group and she began to attend the dances on Friday nights with Ted. Margaret also joined the choir because she loved to sing.

At school, Margaret was fitting in well. Her marks were high and she had many friends but she had trouble reading the blackboard. Miss Webb told Aunt Aileen that Margaret needed glasses, but Auntie was stubborn and refused to do anything about it. Miss Webb moved Margaret to the front of the class.

At Central School, the students could dress any way they liked and Margaret felt out of place wearing her British school uniform every day.

"You can wear some of my clothes, Margaret. I wouldn't mind wearing your uniform skirt. I've always admired it. Maybe we could trade," Jessica offered.

"Thanks, Jessica. That would be great but I'll have to ask my Aunt for new clothes sooner or later."

"Why don't you try talking to Edie Patterson first?" Jessica asked. "You might have more luck with her."

"That's a good idea," Margaret said with relief.

It was early April before she got up the nerve to talk to Mrs. Patterson. Most Saturdays, the Patterson's arrived to take the children on an outing.

One unusually warm day, Jack and Edie took them to Port Colborne for a picnic. Margaret and Beth took off their shoes and stockings to walk barefoot in the rough sand. Tom sat on the dock with his fishing line dangling in the waters of Lake Erie. The lighthouse on the break wall stood off in the distance.

Margaret watched the red bobber dip out of sight beneath the water. Ripples in ever widening circles bounced away from it.

After an hour of fishing, a small perch hung dripping wet from Tom's line. He placed it in a pail by his feet. Margaret watched him throw the line out again with fresh bait and she thought how contented he looked.

Later, Jack Patterson showed Tom how to fillet the perch along with other fish he had caught. They fried them over an open fire.

The girls helped Edie prepare carrots, potatoes and onions by wrapping them in tinfoil and placing them deep under the hot embers to cook. A black pot scoured clean on the inside was filled with boiling water for tea.

After dinner, Jack set up an easel, carefully placed his framed canvas on it, and spread out his painting supplies on a towel. Then he went for a short walk before returning to paint. He found colors in the blue-gray sky and light mixed with shadows on the forest floor. Even the blades of grass seemed to have more shades of brown, yellow and green than Margaret knew existed.

"Where do you see this red color?" Margaret asked pointing. She thought he must have made a mistake.

"Come with me," he took her hand and led her to a spot in the field. A single wild rose bush lurked among the long grasses.

"How did you know it was there?" she asked.

"I have walked here many times so I know where it's growing," he answered. "I walked backward from the rose bush and stopped at a point where I could barely see it and started painting."

Jack and Edie appreciated the small details and surprises life could offer. Margaret wished she could live with them instead of Aunt Aileen.

Jack would be painting for hours and Margaret decided it was a good time to approach Edie alone and discuss her problem. She was not sure if Edie could keep a secret but she knew she would be honest and helpful.

"Mrs. Patterson, I'd like to speak to you about a problem I have, but I don't want you to tell Aunt Aileen I talked to you."

"What's the matter, dear?"

"You may have noticed we're growing taller and our clothes are too small for us. We have no money to buy anything for ourselves."

"Don't worry any more about it. I'll take care of everything," she said, patting Margaret on the back.

CHAPTER 4

A Slap in the Face

Two weeks after Margaret had talked to Edie about her need for clothes, Edie talked to Aunt Aileen.

"You were a generous woman to take the children into your home, Aileen. I'm sorry they don't seem to appreciate it. Why do you let them traipse around in ill-fitting rags bringing shame to your good name?"

"I hadn't considered it. I'll look into the matter immediately."

Margaret decided Auntie was afraid of what people thought of her and wanted to make a good impression. Also, she considered Edie's advice as good as the law.

The next afternoon, Auntie brought back several bags of clothes left over from the Rummage Sale at Holy Trinity Church and dumped them in the laundry room. "Wash these clothes and try them on. Find something decent to wear to school."

Margaret came across several good quality items and, by choosing colors carefully, was able to mix and match some parts of her uniform with other clothes in pleasing combinations. She only hoped the clothes she picked had not been castaways from anyone she knew.

Margaret grew out of her shoes and Auntie bought her a new pair. She put on the ugly shoes and self-consciously walked to school. Some of her girl friends looked at her with pity but Marsha began whispering and pointing at her rudely. Suddenly she marched toward Margaret and stomped down hard on her toes.

Margaret was not the type of person to make a scene but she knew Auntie would hit her if she came home with her shoes scuffed. She glared at Marsha and pushed her down. "Stop it!"

Marsha pounced on Margaret and pulled her hair. Soon they were both rolling around on the grass. When Margaret saw her skirt torn, she pulled her fist back and punched Marsha in the stomach, knocking the wind out of her.

Other kids in the schoolyard were standing around them in a circle and some of the boys were yelling, "Fight!"

Marsha sat up and tried to catch her breath. "I hate your shoes," she said with a nasty voice.

"So do I," Margaret panted.

By the time the teacher arrived, both girls were muddy, their clothes torn, tears running down their cheeks and laughing like crazy.

"Girls, shake hands and go home to change your clothes."

Margaret and Marsha shook hands, "I'm sorry, Margaret".

"Me, too. But what am I going to do? I can't go home to my Aunt looking like this," Margaret said glancing at herself.

"You can wear some of my clothes," Marsha exclaimed. She took Margaret by the arm and they walked to her house to change.

Rose noticed Margaret wearing different clothes and Margaret told her the whole story.

"Come with me and pick out a pair of shoes that you will like. I'll tell Aunt Aileen the shoes she bought you hurt your feet."

Margaret enjoyed trying on many pairs of shoes. A patent leather pair caught her eye. They had buckles and fancy stitching and were pretty enough to dance in. When she saw how expensive they were, she chose a cheaper pair and pointed them out to Rose. But Rose had seen her eyes light up at the more expensive shoes. "Margaret, I think these shoes would suit you better."

"I don't really need them."

"Oh yes you do. They are beautiful shoes and they look lovely on you."

Margaret accepted the new shoes and hid her ugly shoes in the back of the closet. Aunt Aileen frowned but said nothing.

The workload Aunty placed on the children seemed to grow as they grew and the list was twice as long by the time school closed for the summer.

One of Margaret's daily duties was to put the empty glass milk bottles on the front step, pay the milkman and bring the fresh bottles into the house.

The milkman always arrived at the same time riding in a horse-drawn wagon. Margaret started handing him a carrot for his horse every day.

One day the milkman leaned over beside the step and picked one of Aunt Aileen's yellow roses.

"For the lovely lady who feeds my horse," he said, handing it to Margaret.

She was shocked and immediately put it in her apron pocket, "Don't do that again," she whispered. She glanced behind her to see if her Aunt was nearby. The milkman winked at her and whistled his way back to the wagon. Margaret told Beth what had happened.

Unfortunately, the milkman kept pulling Auntie's flowers off until there were none left on the bush. Margaret looked angrily at him whenever he did it but he just grinned.

Aunt Aileen did notice her plant was not keeping its flowers and at first sprayed it with pesticide. Finally, she dug it out and had the bush replaced. She never discovered her error but Margaret and Beth secretly laughed about it whenever the milkman arrived.

Margaret often received letters from her mother and sometimes Auntie would open them before she had a chance to read them. Today, Rose picked up the mail and passed it to Margaret while Margaret was cleaning the bathroom.

Margaret closed the door behind her and sat on the side of the tub. The chores would have to wait. She pulled out the letter and began to read,

Dear Margaret,   *July 16, 1948.*

I received your letter this morning but left it unopened until teatime. I waited until the time you usually get home from school and imagined you were with me, telling me about your day.

I'm happy to know you like school and finished the first year with high marks in most of your subjects.

It sounds like Jessica is a caring friend. She seems concerned with your feelings and interested in your ideas. Your friend Catherine stopped by Aunt Freda's asking about you. She took Aunt Aileen's address and will probably write you a letter.

Jack and Edie took me under their wing when I first came to Canada and I'm pleased to learn they have done the same with you. They treated me as a daughter so I expect they'll treat you like you are their grandchild.

Greet my sister Rose and tell her to behave herself. She enjoys a good joke and you can expect fun whenever she's around.

I have to spend the next three weeks in Barnard Castle Hospital. My Multiple Sclerosis is getting worse and the doctor wants to run some tests. In the near future, I may have to stay here indefinitely.

Aunt Freda, Uncle Charles and baby Gordon come to see me every day. Gordon is growing like a weed. I told him I was writing you a letter and he said to tell you he loves you and to come home soon. Aunt Freda always brings fresh flowers from her garden and raisin scones to eat with my tea.

I miss you and think of you every moment of every day.

Love, Mam

Margaret missed the easy way she could talk to her mother about everything. She put the letter in her pocket and walked to the linen closet for clean towels to hang on the towel rack.

Some afternoons when they finished their chores, Rose played board games with them. She liked to tell them funny stories about their mother when she was young. They were in such high spirits one day that Auntie thought they must have been getting into trouble and sent them to their rooms.

Margaret was turning from a girl to a woman and there were days she wished she could talk to her mother about it. Great Aunt Aileen was too old to remember what it was like, but Rose understood all the feelings and physical changes Margaret was going through.

Margaret often had Migraine headaches. She could barely see to read the recipes in Auntie's cookbooks.

Once during the school year, the teacher had sent her home with a headache. Aunt Aileen met her at the door, slapped her face and sent her back to school. "Little girls don't get headaches," she had said.

Margaret spent the rest of that day with her head down on her desk and her school friends whispering quietly around her.

Today, Margaret was squinting to read a label on a can of peas. Her head was bent over and she kept rubbing her temples.

Rose arrived home from work and immediately took Margaret to her room and laid her on the bed.

Rose checked in on Margaret from time to time.

"What will Auntie do when she finds out I've been sleeping?"

"Don't mention it. Tell her you were helping me clean my room," Aunt Rose responded.

Margaret learned she could trust Rose and talk to her about anything that was bothering her.

That first summer, Margaret's schedule was filled with swimming and tap dancing lessons (thanks to Edie Patterson), piano lessons and babysitting. Margaret was active in the church choir and the Pattersons' continued to take the children out every Saturday. Margaret appreciated how Aunt Rose acted as a buffer between herself and Auntie and she began to think there were many benefits to living in Canada. She was able to get a bicycle, if only to help Auntie deliver parcels, and she often went for a spin just to clear her mind. She spent many hours at the library by herself and stood by the canal watching the lakers and waving to the deck hands. "Maybe someone will recognize me," she thought.

The last day of August, Margaret looked at her small assortment of clothing in disgust. Beth was sitting on her bed watching her. "We're going to need new clothes again, Beth. My clothes aren't worth passing on to you."

"We'll have to ask Auntie," Beth said.

"I'm afraid to ask but she's not going to do anything about it if I don't."

Margaret nervously approached her Aunt and spoke calmly and respectfully. "Aunt Aileen? School will be starting in a week and Beth and I are going to need new clothes."

Aunt Aileen got up from her chair and without warning, swung her hand at the side of Margaret's head, hitting her in the ear. Margaret fell to the hardwood floor with a thud. "Haven't I spent enough of my hard earned money on you children?"

Tom walked into the room and saw Margaret fall. Auntie was about to strike Margaret the second time when Tom ran forward, grabbing her arm. He yanked it back so hard that Auntie flinched. Her eyes watered and her face turned white with anger.

She spun on her heels and marched over to the phone. Her hand was shaking when she picked it up. "Hello," she said in a calm voice, "I'd like to order some train tickets."

Margaret and Tom looked at each other with their eyes wide and mouths hanging open. Auntie was sending Tom back to England.

Margaret's heart sank. She stumbled toward Auntie, "You can't send him away!"

Aunt Aileen hung up the phone. "This is my house! I can do anything I please!" she shouted. Aunt Aileen walked to her bedroom and shut the door.

Margaret stood looking at the closed door. Tom put his arms around her and they both cried for a long time.

Emily Cook (Mam) at Barnard Castle Hospital

CHAPTER 5

Reflections

MARGARET AND BETH were heartbroken when Tom left. Margaret had a hard time concentrating and one night forgot to mix the color into the Oleo Margarine.

Without warning, in the middle of the night, Aunt Aileen yanked Margaret out of bed by her hair.

Margaret stumbled down the stairs to the kitchen where she shakily opened the package of food coloring. Aunt Aileen stood over her for 20 minutes until the work was done and followed her back to her bedroom.

Auntie became increasingly hostile toward Margaret. They tried to avoid each other as much as possible.

Tom's work was divided between the girls and Margaret was given the greater share. Rose helped them as often as she could when Aunt Aileen was out shopping or visiting.

One afternoon, Margaret finished polishing the silver when Aunt Aileen said, "Do them over again."

She finished the silverware for the second time and started washing windows in the sitting room. Auntie stood behind her the whole time, waiting for her to finish. "Do them again."

Margaret hesitated, trying to put her thoughts into words. She knew there was no one to stand up to Aunt Aileen but herself, and she was tired of being bullied by her.

"You've stood over me for the last half hour. When you gave me an order, I followed it to the best of my ability even if I thought you were being unreasonable. I did what you said every time. But I have had enough of your mean ways. This treatment has got to stop. I do what you want me to do and it's not good enough. You tell me not to touch something and then blame me later for not cleaning it."

"Don't you smart mouth me...," her Aunt began.

But Margaret interrupted her and continued to say what was on her mind. "In all the time we have lived here, you've ignored anything we said and treated us as if we don't matter but I insist, you will listen to what I say now."

The phone rang and Auntie got up to answer it.

Margaret raised her voice, "Sit down!"

Auntie did sit down and for a minute Margaret forgot what she was going to say. Her temper soon brought the words back to mind.

"I'm not trying to be disobedient or smart mouth you. I'm tired of your constant criticizing. You are fifty years older than I am. You have much more experience and you do a good job. I don't deny it. But when Beth and I do our very best, and the job is well done, you still find fault with it.

"I plan to follow your rules because it's the right thing to do and I want to honor my mother, but I won't do a job twice if it has been done right the first time. And I won't take the blame for your mistakes."

Margaret marched out of the room. It was the first time she had spoken up to Auntie and she was shaking from the experience.

Auntie stopped talking to Margaret at all and relayed her messages through Beth instead.

Jack and Edie Patterson continued to take the girls on day trips. They frequently asked if the girls had received mail from Tom or their mother, and they discussed the girls' frustrations living with Auntie and their hopes for the future.

Margaret had seen Niagara Falls in the winter time when thick ice covered the trees and bushes and stone fences, even the top of the massive waterfall itself.

She had hiked through the woods in Effingham Park until her legs ached, breathed in the fragrance of cherry blossoms, tasted sap dripping from a maple tree, watched waves crash over the break-wall during a storm and fished from a boat on Lake Erie with only the moon and stars for light.

Her favorite times were when Tom was with them, and after he returned home to England there was something missing from their outings.

On Armistice Day, Jack and Edie Patterson drove everyone to the park to join in the activities. Margaret and Beth sat on a blanket on the grass listening to the drums and bagpipes. Some men spoke about the first and second World Wars and reminded them of their loved ones who had died.

Margaret remembered hiding under her mother's bed with her brothers and sisters while Mam prayed for the soldiers. One building near their childhood home had been destroyed and she remembered the horrible smell of rubber gas masks and the whistle of doodlebugs, a funny name for bombs that stopped whistling just before they blew up.

Aunt Aileen and Edie set out a picnic lunch and everyone sat down to eat. After lunch, Jack went for a walk to talk to some of his friends. Aunt Rose stood and motioned for the girls to follow her. Margaret and Beth walked with Rose along the path. A warm breeze pushed ahead of them and twigs snapped beneath their feet. Autumn was turning green leaves into various shades of yellow, orange and red.

"Aunt Aileen is so mean," Margaret suddenly blurted out. "I don't know how you can stand to live with her, Aunt Rose," Margaret blushed and wished she hadn't said anything.

Aunt Rose smiled. "Aunt Aileen took your mother and I into her home when our mother died and for this we are grateful. She raised us the best she could but never understood our need for affection and has always had a chip on her shoulder. Let me tell you her story."

They stopped by some swings and sat on them. Aunt Rose began, "Aunt Aileen grew up in a family with many brothers and sisters. She was closest in age to her sister Brenda and they were the best of friends.

In those days, a girl was considered bold if she showed interest in a boy and if a young man were interested in a courtship, he would have to ask the girl's father for permission to date her. Most of the time, the only place young people could meet were at dances, church or social activities planned by the local town council.

Aileen and Brenda grew to be teenagers and at the time, there were few young men living in the neighborhood. As fortune would have it, they fell in love with the same man. What made matters worse was he liked them both and couldn't make up his mind about which he liked best. He took turns escorting both of them to social functions.

When World War One started, he joined the army. He promised the girls he would marry one of them after the war but gave them no indication which one. Neither girl was willing to give him to the other and they waited, knowing his choice would probably drive them apart.

The sisters sent him notes and parcels through the mail but they went unanswered. Eventually, a letter came listing him as missing in action.

Aileen and Brenda were so overcome with grief they could not face each other. Aileen moved to Canada and they have not spoken to each other since. Neither one has ever married."

"But what has that got to do with how she treats us?" Margaret asked.

"Aunt Aileen spends her time as counselor at your school. She runs a well-respected boarding house and takes time to help her friends. I think you children remind her of the youth she's trying to forget. She has tried to bury her feelings by being busy and I think she can only express them when she's angry."

After this, Margaret went out of her way to be considerate to her Aunt and even though Auntie wouldn't acknowledge her efforts, she began to lessen their restrictions.

Auntie bought her first television and on Friday nights she invited the girls to sit on the floor in the living room to watch it. One night, Margaret asked Aunt Aileen if Ted could join them and she agreed. Ted started to arrive every Friday night to watch T.V. with them and soon became a normal part of the routine. Auntie expected him to show up and if he didn't she became very upset.

One night, all the boarders were out. Aunt Rose was working and Beth was visiting a friend.

"Margaret?" Aunt Aileen said, "Tonight you will come with me to play Bingo."

"I wonder if she's afraid to leave me alone in the house," Margaret thought as she changed into a clean dress.

Margaret was amazed to see Auntie wearing a gorgeous fur coat. She usually wore a straight-lined gray skirt and plain white blouse and a cardigan sweater as if it were a uniform.

Jack whistled when he saw Aileen and Edie said, "Stop that."

Aunt Aileen blushed and waved him off, pretending not to care what he did. This unexpected reaction was in loud contrast to her usual stone-faced manner. Margaret wondered if she had been drinking.

The Bingo Hall was lit with bright lights. Rows of tables and chairs faced the front. Jack went to buy game cards. Soon the night began. Margaret didn't mind the game, except her Aunt was constantly telling her what to do on one side and Edie was telling her just the opposite from the other side. Besides the fact, there were no other young people present. She'd rather have been dancing with Ted or watching a movie with Jessica.

The next time her Aunt told Margaret she had to come to Bingo, Margaret said she couldn't possibly go since she had too much to do.

Aunt Aileen never asked her to come to Bingo after that.

Margaret, Uncle Jack and Beth at the park

CHAPTER 6

Picking Cherries

MARGARET COMPLETED HER first year at Welland High School. It was the summer of 1951 and she was 15 years old. Margaret stood beside the sink, scrubbing a stubborn burn on a well-used frying pan. Her hair had come undone and was getting into her eyes and beads of sweat were dripping down her forehead.

Aunt Aileen walked into the kitchen, "Margaret? As soon as you turn 16 in October I expect you to get a job and move out."

Without waiting for a reply, she turned and walked away.

Margaret had barely enough time to stammer, "Whaa..!"

She stood there with her mouth hanging open and her face drained of color. "What about school?" she muttered to herself. "Who will hire a young girl like me? I've tried to make money doing odd jobs but Auntie has taken every cent."

Margaret was desperate to find work. She finished the dishes, hung up the dish towel and put away the cleaning supplies before going upstairs to talk to Rose.

"Aunt Rose, I don't know what to do. In four months I have to move out."

"What do you mean?"

Margaret proceeded to tell Aunt Rose what Aunt Aileen said.

Aunt Rose frowned, "Try not to let it bother you tonight."

She motioned Margaret to come over and gave her a big hug.

"It's best to keep working on your chores. I'll see what I can do to help. It's no use trying to change her mind."

Rose helped Margaret save a little money and keep it hidden from Aunt Aileen. She used some of her own money to help Margaret purchase underclothes and personal products. When Auntie questioned her about new things, Rose instantly came to her defense and claimed she bought it for Margaret. Auntie accused her of spoiling the girls but it kept her off their backs.

As Margaret's 16th birthday came closer, she became concerned that the little amount of money she had saved wouldn't be enough. Aunt Rose convinced Aunt Aileen that Margaret should go cherry picking with her in order to bring more money into the house.

From this point on, Margaret was no longer expected to do chores as long as she brought home enough money to satisfy Auntie. Rose told Aunt Aileen that Margaret was working for a certain amount of money, but actually Margaret was going to be paid more. Rose put the extra money away in a safe place where Aunt Aileen couldn't find it, so in this way the money Margaret was able to save grew much larger.

The first day of her new job, Margaret woke to her alarm clock at 4:00 a.m. She tried to make as little noise as possible. She tiptoed out of her room, and without turning a light on, carried her clothes to the washroom. She took a bath and got dressed, brushed her teeth and tied her hair back with a silk scarf.

She made her way downstairs. Rose was buttering toast and pouring tea into cups for their breakfast. "Good morning, Margaret. Here's a cup of tea and some toast with a slice of Swiss cheese."

"Thank you," she said, taking the warm cup and setting it down on the kitchen table. She bit into the toast hungrily.

Together, they cleared the table and prepared a basket lunch and a thermos of hot tea.

They walked a half-mile to the trolley car on Prince Charles Drive and then, when they arrived in Fonthill, they had to walk several miles up a gravel road to the orchard. They passed a dairy farm where a sprinkling of Holstein cows dotted a field.

Across the road, workers in a vineyard were tending rows of grapevines.

The light of dawn crept up in the East and the cool air was crisp. Margaret's shoes and stockings were damp with dew. Once the sun rose, she began to dry off.

Rose pointed toward a red brick building. A young woman stood on tiptoe pinning clothes to a line while a dog and small child tumbled over each other at her feet.

"There's the farmer," Rose commented.

The proprietor of the cherry orchard was a tall, thin, gray haired gentleman wearing coveralls. He stood slightly stooped over beside his tractor and motioned with his arm for the girls to hurry.

Margaret and Rose climbed onto a flat wagon loaded with baskets, hitched to the tractor. Other workers sat around talking to each other. "Hi, Rose."

"This is my niece Margaret," she said.

The workers introduced themselves. A couple people offered a friendly handshake before turning away to continue talking with someone else.

The farmer drove the tractor into the orchard, depositing baskets and letting groups of workers off in various locations. Margaret and Aunt Rose were the last to get off. It was a bumpy ride over ruts and clumps of dry grass. The farmer stopped the tractor and got out. He set some baskets beside a tree.

His face was lined with age and Margaret worried about his safety when he climbed an old wooden ladder to show her how to reach the best cherries. He swung himself down from the tree with an agility he acquired from many years of hard work. "He's stronger than I thought," Margaret thought with surprise.

Some of the surprise must have shown on her face for he smiled when he saw her expression.

"Start at this tree and work your way down the row. When your baskets are full, start at the next tree. Move the ladder along as you go and pick only the ripest cherries. "See," he reached up and picked a cherry, showing it to Margaret. "These cherries are starting to split. They'll be used for jam and need to be picked right away. You don't want any other cherries to become this ripe. I can lose a great deal of money if they're picked too late. Pick them before they get to this stage. Rose will show you what to do.

"Eat as many as you like, but they've been sprayed and need to be washed first. Remember, you're only paid for the number of baskets you pick and the quality of your work so don't waste your time or mine."

With that long-winded speech, he was off with his tractor depositing baskets along every few trees or so.

"What do we do once the baskets are full?" Margaret asked.

"Don't worry, he'll be back with his wagon. We'll work in our section until he tells us he wants us working somewhere else."

They picked cherries for several hours without talking before they sat down for a thermos of tea and a sandwich. It was still early morning but Margaret was feeling hungry. They were starting on a second tree when the farmer arrived to pick up the full baskets. He looked pleased at the number of baskets and quality of the cherries that filled them.

Margaret had been careful not to put any with splits, worms or mould in the baskets.

The farmer came toward them, "There's a tree I'd like picked today 3 rows East and 25 Rows North. I want you two to be the ones to pick it. Hop on the wagon and I'll give you a lift."

After he left, Rose commented, "He doesn't usually go out of his way to help any of us. He tells us where to go and we have to walk there. I think he was surprised at how well you picked today so far, and he was letting you know he was pleased with your work. When I first asked if you could work with me, he didn't think it was a good idea because you are so young. I think he expected we would spend all our time talking instead of working. I knew I could depend on you, Margaret. I'm proud of how well you're doing."

Margaret was happy Aunt Rose was proud of her. She decided to work even harder at doing a good job. At the end of the first day she was feeling tired and sore but satisfied that she'd done her best. By 5:00 p.m., she and Rose had picked as many baskets of good cherries as some of the farmer's regular hired workers.

"I'll be happy to employ you for the rest of the summer, Margaret. You're a good worker," the farmer shook Margaret's hand and nodded at Rose before leaving them and walked away to attend to other matters.

This was not the end of Margaret's workday. After they left the farm, they worked from 6:00 p.m. until 11:00 at the canning factory. Margaret started to get sleepy after working in the fresh air all day and standing up for four more hours canning cherries.

During the walk back to town to catch the trolley, Aunt Rose kept Margaret awake telling her funny stories about her mother's childhood. She dozed off while sitting in the streetcar but they still had to walk half a mile. It was close to midnight when they arrived home.

Margaret fell asleep dreaming of cherries. In four hours, it was time to get up and start over again.

At the end of the first week, she was exhausted but slowly her body adjusted to the demanding schedule. She watched her few dollars grow into a surprising amount of money and decided it was worth the trouble. She worked from Monday to Friday and on weekends she went dancing or to the show with her friends. After the cherry season, she picked peaches.

Aunt Rose as a nurse during the war

CHAPTER 7

A Companion

MARGARET WAS SORRY she could not return to High School in September, but Rose found a suitable job for her as a live-in companion for Mrs. Smith. Mrs. Smith was an elderly woman confined to a wheelchair by Arthritis. She and her family owned a lumberyard. They were friends of Aunt Rose.

After being introduced to Mrs. Smith, Rose helped Margaret carry her suitcases up an outside staircase to the second story bachelor apartment. Mrs. Smith's granddaughter Cathy followed behind with a key to unlock the door.

As soon as Margaret stepped into the neat little room, her face lit up. There was a kitchen nook, an armchair, a small washroom and a little bed with matching dressers. White curtains covered a single window that was open, allowing fresh air into the room, and the bedding was white with embroidered purple lilies.

There was a little radio on the nightstand and an excellent view from the one window beside the door. The area behind the house was forested and the leaves were starting to change to their autumn colors. Margaret was thrilled.

"I'll leave you alone, to get used to your place and I'll stop by tomorrow to check on you. Are you going to be all right?" Rose asked.

"I'll be fine. It's such a beautiful apartment, Aunt Rose. It's perfect!"

After unpacking, Margaret climbed between the new sheets and slept soundly.

She woke to the sound of her alarm and became excited when she remembered where she was. "I'd better not be late for breakfast." She rushed to get ready and put on her white blouse and yellow jumper.

When she arrived downstairs, Cathy's father was already seated at the table with his sons Don and Carl. He stood and pulled out a chair for her, "Come sit here, Margaret."

Soon Mrs. Smith and Cathy joined them from the kitchen. Cathy set dishes of food down on the table and everyone began passing Margaret toast, jam, sausages, cheese, eggs, fried tomatoes, hash browns, and tea. She was amazed at the amount of food there was and how quickly it was gone.

Margaret took one piece of toast, some cheese and an egg.

"Are you ill, my Dear?" Mrs. Smith inquired with concern.

"Oh, no. This is more food than I usually eat in the morning. I'm quite well. Thank you."

Cathy looked surprised at the small amount of food on Margaret's plate. "No wonder she has such a nice figure."

Don looked at Margaret with interest, "She does seem to keep herself fit."

When Mr. Smith also agreed, Margaret blushed.

After breakfast, the table was cleared of dirty dishes. The men left the house in record time. Carl was the last one out and he winked at Margaret before closing the door behind him.

Mrs. Smith put Margaret at ease. "You have nothing to fear from my grandson's, Margaret. They are all gentlemen."

Cathy had a three-year-old daughter named Susie who followed

Margaret around like a shadow. Cathy carried her out of the room so Mrs. Smith could talk to Margaret.

"Well, Margaret. I see my family has accepted you and Susie is in love with you. However, I hope you won't become bored since you were hired to keep me company. Rose tells me you have experience looking after an invalid."

"Yes, my mother. She has Multiple Sclerosis and her legs have been paralyzed since I was a young child. I have cared for her along with my brothers and sisters. I mean we all took care of her and each other."

"Your Aunt Rose recommends you highly saying you have much experience in cooking and cleaning."

"As you know, Great Aunt Aileen owns a boarding house. We learned different ways to cook and clean while at home as well as under Aunt Aileen's instruction."

"Rose says you weren't happy living with your Aunt Aileen. What if you aren't happy living with me?"

"I can assure you I'll work to the best of my ability and if you find I'm not up to your standards, I'll gladly change what I'm doing to please you.

"If for some reason I find I'm not happy in this job, I'll let you know in enough time to find a replacement and give my reasons as honestly as I can."

"Then, Margaret, welcome to the family. I believe we will get along famously. You can bring any problems you have to me and we will work things out.

"Today, if you'd like to help me bake cookies, we can give Susie a surprise with her tea. Afterward, perhaps you could read something to me from the Holy Scriptures. I understand you are a religious person."

"I'd be happy to," Margaret replied.

Margaret worked comfortably at her new job in the Smith's home. Don and Carl treated her as a sister and teased her the way they teased Cathy. Sometimes, Cathy and Margaret joined forces and pulled a prank or two on the boys just for fun.

She spent some of her spare time making a dollhouse for Susie. She created and decorated furniture out of matchboxes and paper dolls with different outfits Susie could dress them in.

On Friday nights, if Don or Carl had to drive into town for supplies, they would often give her a lift to Auntie's house. She would stay overnight with Beth, go out with her friends on Saturday and Jack Patterson would drive her back to the Smith's Sunday night.

Margaret knew Aunt Aileen did not want her sleeping over but she paid Aunt Rose for the room like any other boarder and stayed out of sight as much as possible. In this way, Aunt Aileen tolerated her visits.

On Halloween night, Margaret and Beth borrowed swimwear from Edie Patterson. The suits were from the 1930's, reaching from ankle to neck and made of striped flannel. Margaret modeled her swimsuit for Mrs. Smith and she laughed out loud at the sight.

"My mother used to wear a swimsuit like that," she gasped.

At that moment, Cathy entered the room. "Margaret, would you like to go with Susie and I trick-or-treating? I'm planning to take her out from 7:00 p.m. to 8:00. What kind of an outfit is that?"

"I'd love to go," Margaret answered. "and it's a swimsuit. Later in the evening, I'll be going to a Halloween party at Jessica's."

"I'll drop you off after we go out with Susie," Cathy offered. "Do you think you can arrange a ride home?"

"If I can't, I'll stay overnight and get a ride up on the Trolley in the morning."

Cathy dressed Susie in a clown outfit. Susie kept pulling her red nose off so they tied it on with a string.

Susie ran around Margaret and bounced off the sofa, nearly knocking over a lamp. Cathy grabbed her and tickled her. When she calmed down, Cathy let go of her and she pulled off her nose again.

"You have to keep it on if you want people to think you're a real clown," she said.

Susie kept pushing it away, "Too hot."

Once they got in the car, she put her nose back on without any trouble. She was very excited as they drove into town, and kept bouncing up and down on the seat.

After they parked the car, she ran to the first house but stopped short when a big ghost walked by.

Margaret told Susie, "Don't be afraid. He's just dressed like a ghost. He's really a big boy with a pillowcase getting candy like you."

"Not like me," Susie said. "I'm a clown."

Cathy lifted Susie high enough to reach the doorbell of the first house and a lady answered the door.

"Hello. Are you a clown?"

"NO!" she shouted. "I'm Susie!" She pulled off her nose. "See? This is pretend."

"Oh, now I see you Susie. Would you like some candy?"

"Trick or treat," said Susie opening her bag and putting her thumb in her mouth.

The lady laughed and put a large handful of candy in the bag.

"I don't like peanuts," Susie said mournfully.

"Well, I do," Cathy exclaimed grabbing Susie's hand.

"Thank you very much."

The lady was still laughing as she served a young skeleton who arrived next at her door.

Cathy walked quickly away with Susie protesting, "I don't! I don't want any!"

They went from door to door for almost an hour. Some of the homes were decorated with orange and black decorations, spider webs and big rubber spiders, pictures of witches and goblins. Susie was most interested in the amount of candy she was accumulating and the different faces carved into the pumpkins.

After they saw a pumpkin almost as big as Susie with a very funny face, Margaret expected Susie to say something about it.

Susie looked at the pumpkin and said, "I have to go to the bathroom."

Cathy decided it was time to go home. She dropped Margaret off at Aunt Aileen's to freshen up.

Margaret knocked on the door and Aunt Rose answered. "Hi, Margaret. Aren't you a sight! Beth is just about ready. Come in and sit down."

Aunt Rose brought Margaret a cookie. It still seemed strange to come here as a visitor.

Beth came down stairs. "Bye, Aunt Rose."

"Bye girls. Don't stay out too late."

Margaret and Beth walked to Jessica's house.

The table was set with decorative plates and napkins. Refreshments included root-beer and orange pop, coffee and tea, cupcakes with orange icing, popcorn and taffy-apples.

Ray, a friend of Tom, asked Margaret to dance.

Margaret wasn't attracted to Ray but she did want to dance so she accepted. He was dressed as Frankenstein's monster and it suited him. He danced like a mannequin, as stiff as a board.

Different party games had been arranged. Teams were picked and the winners were awarded gag prizes.

Ted arrived half way through the party and came to sit beside Margaret. They got up together and walked to the table for snacks.

Margaret hadn't seen Ted since she left school in June. "It's nice to see you Ted. How have you been keeping?"

"Well, I was employed by my Uncle at his farm for the summer. Now school has started, I work weekends at a service station pumping gas. I've missed you, Margaret. Would you consider going out to dinner with me some time?"

"Of course! I'd love to!"

The party ended early. Jessica's mother was grateful and surprised by how quickly the food and dirty dishes were cleared and the room straightened.

It was a cool night for a walk, but the partygoers, still dressed in their costumes, headed toward the theatre to watch King Kong. Beth had won her theatre ticket as a prize for the best costume.

At first the attendant was unsure about whether to let them in but Jessica took off her mask and identified herself, naming each of her friends.

After midnight, Margaret arrived back at her apartment. It had been a good night and she slept peacefully.

Early the next morning, Aunt Aileen had a stroke. Aunt Rose called and left a message for Margaret.

Aunt Aileen was partially paralyzed and unable to talk but the doctor thought it was not too severe and had good hope she would regain her strength and her speech in the coming months.

Margaret was not sure what she was going to do. "I'm afraid my sister Beth may have to quit school in order to look after Auntie," she explained to Mrs. Smith. "I love my new job and I don't want to leave but I think it's my duty to help Beth look after her.

"I was talking to Aunt Rose and she said Auntie needs special nursing care. Aunt Rose can't afford to give up her full time position to stay at home and Auntie refuses to go to a hospital or pay for a nurse to come to the house."

"I'm sorry you have to leave, Margaret. But I'm pleased to see you care for your family. Your job will be here when you return."

Margaret & Beth at a dock in Port Colborne

CHAPTER 8

The Party

MARGARET ARRIVED AT Auntie's and Beth took her upstairs to one of the guest rooms. Margaret reached into her purse and took out some money.

"Put this in an envelope and give it to Aunt Aileen when she's feeling better."

"You shouldn't have to pay for your room, Margaret."

"I want to. It will keep Auntie from feeling angry after she finds out I'm here."

Beth noticed an old towel draped over the back of a chair and bent over to pick it up.

"Don't worry about cleaning my room for me, Beth. I've done it hundreds of times myself and know what's expected," she reached over and took the towel from her.

"It's good to have you back, Margaret. I've missed your company."

"I've missed you too," she said and gave Beth a hug.

"I think I'll go down and let her know I'm here," Margaret said.

Margaret walked down the back stairs to Aunt Aileen's bedroom. The door was unlocked, making it easier to carry clean linen and toiletries to her room.

Margaret tapped lightly on Auntie's door and looked inside. She was sitting up with pillows supporting her back. She looked at Margaret and frowned, "Other stairs."

"Don't be ridiculous," Margaret answered. "I'm here to help so Rose can keep her job and Beth can stay in school."

During the weeks and months Margaret looked after Auntie, she examined the photographs in her room. "Who are the young girls in this old photo, Aunt Aileen?"

"Brenda," Aunt Aileen managed to say.

Many of the photographs were of Aunt Aileen and her sister in their youth but there were no recent photographs after that.

Margaret thought, "It's about time Aunt Aileen has something to smile about. I have an idea that just might work."

Since the summer, Margaret had saved enough money to buy a one-way ticket to Britain and was trying to save enough to travel with Beth to visit their mother. But since Aunt Aileen was old, she thought her mother would live many more years and decided to use the money to bring Aunt Brenda to Canada.

"Aunt Aileen, when you are feeling better, we're going to have a Christmas Party."

"No," Aunt Aileen grunted.

"Nonsense," Margaret countered. "I'll talk to Aunt Rose and we'll plan it right away."

As soon as Aileen was able to speak, she let them know in no uncertain terms that she was opposed to the idea. However, as she regained her strength, she also became more interested. "Well, you're going to have your own way no matter what I say. I can sit in my chair," she said, giving in to the idea. Immediately, she started to take over the planning.

"Why do you have to spend money on a new punch bowl? Why are you inviting so many people? I wish you'd let me decide who should come to my party."

Jack Patterson bought a pine tree and the girls and Rose decorated it with candles and popcorn strings and bright colorful tinsel. Holly and ivy were hung over doorways and dishes of candy were placed on every flat surface. Rose opened a bottle of homemade wine from the cellar.

Aunt Aileen signed her name to invitations before the guest list was complete.

"I'll fill in the information later," Rose explained. In this way, Rose made it possible for Margaret to send one of the invitations to Aunt Brenda, inviting her to the party, giving her the name of a travel agent to contact and enough money to cover the expenses of her journey.

If Rose and the girls made preparations for the party that deviated from Aunt Aileen's expectations, they were forced to abandon them for more formal ideas: Auntie fussed and complained constantly but Margaret didn't mind. Auntie could have the party as boring as she liked.

As the invitations were received, many people replied by mail. Aunt Rose intercepted the one from Aunt Brenda and took it upstairs. She read it to Margaret and Beth.

> *Dear Aileen,*
>
> *I was so happy to receive such an open invitation. My heart has ached for the many years we have been apart. Thank you for reaching out to me in this way. I look forward to seeing you at the party. Merry Christmas.*
>
> *Love Brenda.*

Margaret clapped her hands, "Great!"

The day of the party, Margaret and Beth set out tea, coffee, and trays of sandwiches, pickles and other finger foods on the dining room table. Fancy glass dishes with cookies, squares and cakes were waiting in preparation on the kitchen table.

Chairs were positioned around the walls of the sitting room as well as the dining room to accommodate guests.

Margaret and Aunt Rose helped Aunt Aileen into her favorite armchair and propped pillows around her to make her comfortable. They set the table with good china and silverware.

"Use the white tablecloth with the gold trim and the matching napkins," Aunt Aileen told them. "You'll find them in the bottom drawer of the china cabinet."

The girls reset the table in time for the first guests to arrive. Beth took their coats and Margaret walked them into the sitting room.

Aunt Aileen greeted them from her armchair. She received extra attention and sympathy from friends she had not seen in a while. Many talked to her about their own ailments and she seemed to enjoy giving them advice.

Margaret kept an eye on the clock, waiting for the time Jack and Edie would arrive with the surprise.

When Jack arrived, he opened the door and handed his hat and coat to Beth. "Hello, Aileen. We were driving by the train station when we saw something we thought might interest you."

"Stop speaking in riddles. What do you mean? Why are you standing like that? You look like a boy caught stealing apples."

Jack blushed at this and stepped back out of sight. There was a great deal of whispering and it looked to Margaret like Aunt Aileen might lose her temper if it wasn't for her great curiosity. Edie entered the room followed by a white haired woman who resembled Aunt Aileen.

"Brenda?" Aileen whispered.

"Aileen!"

Aileen rose unsteadily to her feet and motioned for Brenda to follow her into her bedroom. Aunt Brenda took Aileen's arm and helped her to the bedroom, closing the door behind them.

"What do we do now?" Beth wondered.

"Turn on the Victrola," Margaret suggested.

Once the music started to play, the guests relaxed. Some were sitting and chatting together, some eating and some had moved their chairs back and were dancing to the quiet music.

Jack Patterson approached Margaret and cornered her at the entrance to the kitchen. "Aileen didn't send her sister an invitation, did she Margaret?"

"No, Beth and I planned it with help from Rose," Margaret admitted.

"Brenda could not believe what a change must have come over her sister and was thrilled to think she could see her at last. But I'm concerned with the outcome of their meeting in this way. It might not be the right time, although I think they have been separated long enough. I only hope their love is strong enough to allow themselves to forgive each other."

Margaret looked with concern at the closed door and listened to hear any raised voices or signs of trouble but to her relief, when the door opened and the two sisters walked out, Aunt Aileen had the hint of a smile on her face.

Aileen sat beside Brenda and they talked all evening. Aileen looked off into the distance at times and Margaret thought she must have been reliving a moment in her past.

One by one the guests departed, shaking Aunt Aileen's hand or leaving her with a kind word.

"It was a lovely evening."

"Thank you, for the invitation."

"I hope we can do this again soon."

Margaret and Beth washed and put away the dishes. Edie tidied the sitting room while Aunt Rose changed the bed sheets in the spare bedroom in preparation for Great Aunt Brenda's stay.

Margaret packed up her own things and prepared to move back to her apartment in Fonthill.

"Aunt Aileen, I've called Mrs. Smith. She'll be expecting me. I hope your health continues to improve and you enjoy your visit with Brenda."

"Somehow, I knew you'd be at the bottom of this. You always act before you think about the consequences. Even if your intentions were good; the results could have been disastrous. The shock at seeing Brenda after so many years may have triggered another stroke. We may have remained angry at each other anyway and you would have spent your money for nothing. I didn't realize you would be making so much at the Smith's but that's beside the point. It is only because of our good upbringing and the willingness to forgive each other that everything turned out for the best. I have invited Brenda to stay as long as she wants and she has agreed to help me at the boarding house until I am back on my feet again," Aunt Aileen paused to reflect on what she just said. "Thank you, Margaret."

Margaret was startled by this sudden appreciation. "Good-bye Auntie," Margaret said.

"Go on then. No one's stopping you," Aunt Aileen sounded like she was losing her composure so she stopped talking abruptly and turned away.

Margaret leaned over and kissed her on the cheek.

She walked over to Aunt Rose and gave her a hug. Then she put on her coat and leather boots.

Jack Patterson picked up her luggage and carried it out to his car.

"I'll come with you," Beth remarked, slipping on her boots.

Jack kept up a continuous flow of conversation without pausing to let the girls answer any of his questions. They had never heard him talk so much. Margaret supposed this was because he seldom went anywhere without Edie and she usually dominated the conversation. It could also be the shot of rum in his coffee he allowed himself at the end of the party.

"It was a blessing when you children arrived in Welland. You'll be missed no matter what Aileen says to the contrary. Margaret, I wish you well at your new job. Call on us from time to time."

"I will," she promised.

Jack drove the car into the long driveway and turned the motor off. He got out and opened the car door for the girls.

"Why don't you come up to the house and meet the Smiths, Uncle Jack?" Margaret asked as she climbed out of the back seat.

"I'll just wait here until Beth returns, Margaret. Perhaps the next time I'm here I'll go in with you." He took Margaret by the shoulders and pulled her close, kissing her forehead. He remained standing beside the car and took a cigar from his jacket pocket and lit it. Aunt Edie wouldn't let him smoke when she was around so he was taking advantage of the moment.

Margaret and Beth walked to the house and Margaret rang the doorbell. She didn't wait for someone to come to the door but walked right in.

"Margaret's home!" Susie shouted as she ran from the kitchen. Margaret put down her suitcase and braced herself for a big hug. Susie ran toward her and jumped into her arms.

"Are you home to stay?" she asked anxiously.

"Yes, Susie. Meet my sister Beth. She'll come to visit us sometimes."

Susie was too shy to say anything to Beth.

Mrs. Smith had been watching the girls from the kitchen doorway.

"Hello, Margaret. We've missed you. Welcome Beth. Come and visit your sister anytime."

"Thank you, Mrs. Smith."

"The housekeeper has just cleaned your room so it's ready for you to move back in, Margaret." She wheeled her chair over to Margaret and took a key out of her apron pocket.

Margaret gave Mrs. Smith a hug and took the key, motioning for Beth to follow her out the door. Susie climbed on the sofa and pushed back the curtains to watch Margaret and Beth climb the outside stairs to her apartment. Margaret noticed her little nose pressed against the glass and waved. She saw Susie laughing excitedly.

"You're sure you won't change your mind, Beth. I wasn't kidding when I said the Smith's treat me like one of the family. Susie thinks I'm her big sister."

"No, I'll be fine with Aunt Aileen and Aunt Rose. There are only a few more years before I'll be on my own too. Aunt Rose will be getting married in the summer. What do you think of that? With Aunt Brenda staying on, I think I'll concentrate on my schooling and future plans," Beth hugged her and climbed back down the stairs.

Jack butted out his cigar and opened the passenger door for Beth to get in. He walked back to the driver's side and climbed in himself. They both waved as they backed out of the driveway and headed down the road.

"I'm sure Beth will manage. She has certainly grown up over the last four years," she thought. She turned the key in the lock and opened the door to her apartment.

She hung her coat on a hook, and put her suitcase down at the entrance. Feeling very tired, she dove for the bed and flopped down, planting her face in the fluffy pillow. "I'll just close my eyes for a second," she thought.

Margaret at Pt. Dalhousie

CHAPTER 9

Sweet Dreams

CHANGES WERE MADE at Aunt Aileen's boarding house after the arrival of Aunt Brenda. She decided to stay indefinitely.

Beth had more free time since Great Aunt Brenda insisted on taking over some of the chores to pay her way while in Canada.

After the Christmas Party, there seemed to be more visitors to see the two sisters and some old friendships were rekindled.

When Margaret came to visit Beth, she noticed the place seemed less stuffy and a bit more cheerful. Aunt Aileen's expression seemed softer and an occasional smile made her more approachable.

Margaret thought back over the three years spent at Auntie's. It had been difficult but she had learned skills at a younger age than most and would have no trouble taking care of herself or Beth if it became necessary.

One thing Margaret promised herself, if she ever got married and had children, she would try to make their little lives fun and if they had to do chores, she would make it into a game so they would not mind helping. "If I have a home of my own I'll fill it with happiness and if I have a garden, I'll fill it with flowers," she thought.

Working at the Smiths' was a blessing at first but her workload tripled when Cathy had her second child.

After she returned from the hospital, Cathy was unable to get around. She was very weak and the doctor had recommended bed rest. So, Margaret had to look after Mrs. Smith, baby-sit little Susie, and play nursemaid to Cathy. She was starting to get tired and requested a month vacation. She packed her suitcase and moved back to Aunt Aileen's as a boarder for the month of June. Auntie treated her tolerably well provided she paid for her room and board on time. She began seeing more of Ted and Auntie didn't seem to mind if he came over for meals occasionally.

Margaret received a letter one day near the end of June from Mam. She put it down and covered her face with her hands and cried. Beth was in her own room reading and Margaret knocked on her bedroom door. "Would you like to go to Cross Street Pool?"

"Sure! Let's pack a picnic lunch."

The girls put their swimsuits on under their shorts and tops. Margaret tucked Mam's letter in her pocket. She needed someone to talk to and Beth was always a good listener.

Beth and Margaret walked to the Cross Street pool and spread out a blanket and picnic lunch beside it. Beth went swimming first while Margaret stayed with their belongings. The water was cool, fed by the canal that ran parallel to it, and the cement steps leading down into the water were slippery.

Beth climbed down carefully to the water's edge before diving into the shallow water. The summer sun was warm and when Beth came out, Margaret took a turn. The water was refreshing after she got in but it took her breath away at first. She swam lengths until she was tired, climbed out of the pool and wrapped a towel around her waist. She sat on the grass beside Beth and rubbed some lotion on her shoulders. "I think I'm getting a sunburn," she remarked. "We should probably sit under that shade tree."

Beth picked up the blanket and spread it out under the tree. She opened the cooler and handed a tomato and cheese sandwich to Margaret. It was cold and tasted good. Margaret poured a cup of iced tea from a thermos and handed it to Beth. She then poured some for herself.

"Aunt Rose gave me this last night. I opened it at breakfast this morning," she said holding Mam's letter.

Beth reached for it and started to read.

"It's not fair. Mam is too young to be put in a hospital," Beth remarked sadly.

Margaret looked at the playground in the park. "Remember when we used to take Mam out in her wheelchair and push her around the park, taking turns sitting beside her under the shade trees?"

"She loved to watch us play tag or swing on the swings," Beth remarked.

"She'll be forced to stay indoors surrounded by the smell of medicine and sick people," Margaret choked.

Beth read more of the letter, "Tom has joined the army. I wonder what that's all about. I suppose he'll be paid well and it gives him a job and a home, but what if there's another war?" Beth looked worried.

"And what about Gordon?" He'll soon be eight years old. He'll grow up without knowing who his brothers and sisters are."

Beth and Margaret spent the rest of the afternoon talking about their family and how much they had missed in the four years they had lived in Canada.

"I wish I could bring Mam and baby Gordon to live with us in Canada," Margaret said.

"Mam explained in her letter the reasons she can't be moved. The doctor told her it would only make her condition worse," Beth said sadly.

"I feel helpless, unable to do anything for our family. All I want is for them to be happy and for us all to be together," Margaret said. She drank the rest of her tea.

Beth reached out a hand to Margaret, "I feel the same way."

Margaret put the letter in her pocket and the conversation turned to more cheerful topics. Beth had a new boyfriend and she told Margaret all about him.

"He has a cousin, Margaret. I think you will really like him."

"I already have a boyfriend," Margaret responded.

Beth talked excitedly about how nice Frank's cousin was.

"Why don't you go out with him?" Margaret teased.

"You know how much I love Frank, but you and Ted aren't that serious yet and you know it never hurts to look around."

"You're silly," Margaret said. "If it makes you happy, I suppose I can meet him once but I think Ted will be jealous."

"Good," Beth answered.

"Good what? That I will meet Frank's cousin or that Ted will be jealous?"

Beth didn't answer but looked like she had a secret.

"What's the matter?"

"Nothing."

They sat looking out over the park and talked for a long time. Yellow buttercups and dandelions were scattered around the grass and a bumblebee flew close to the girls. Beth ducked and Margaret got up and moved until it flew away. One lone seagull called at them mournfully for a piece of bread so they gave it to him. Suddenly there were three and the girls had to put the rest of their lunch away. They moved their blanket closer to the pool. A cicada started buzzing, loud enough to be heard over the laughter and shouting of other park visitors.

"This is a noisy place," Margaret said. When Beth didn't answer, she flicked a little piece of bread at Beth. Something was holding Beth's attention and when Margaret looked up, she saw what must be Beth's boyfriend walking toward them.

"Did you tell him we would be here?"

Beth nodded.

Standing beside her boyfriend was his cousin.

Margaret couldn't take her eyes off him. "You should have warned me," she said.

Beth whispered, "Didn't I tell you his cousin was dreamy?"

"Hi, Beth," Frank leaned over and gave her a kiss on the cheek. "Is this your sister?"

"Yes, this is Margaret."

"Hi, Margaret," he said. "This is my cousin Ed."

Margaret looked at the handsome young man and his black curly hair and instantly felt a connection. "This is the man I'm going to marry!" she thought with growing excitement.

"Hello, Margaret," he said.

Edward

ISBN 142518668-8